Bethany's Betrothal

By Sarah Lynn Shade

Dedicated to my parents,
Dale and Brenda Shade, who personally
experienced a Divine betrothal.

ISBN 0-9788703-0-1

All Scripture quotations are taken from the Holy Bible, King James Version.

This is a work of fiction. Names, characters, and plot line are products of the author's imagination. Any resemblance to real people, living or dead, is purely coincidental.

Printed By:

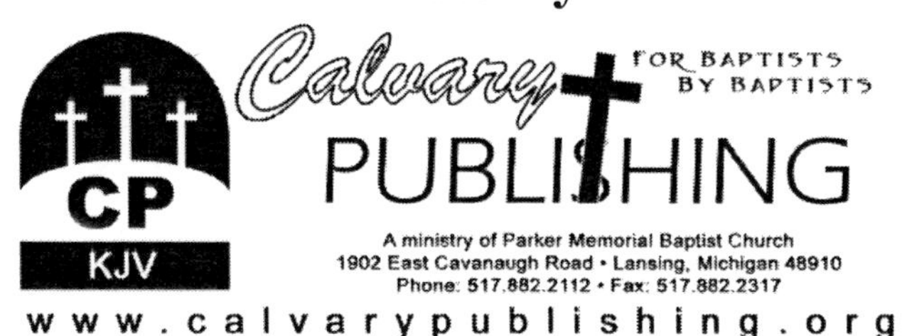

For more copies, visit:
www.localchurchbiblepublishers.com

Also available in the Divine Betrothal Series

Linda the Loser $5.00

Unlike her prospering and successful friends, Linda is required to remain at home and serve under her dad's watchful eye until the day her hand is given away in marriage. She feels like such a loser. Who would ever want to marry her? Linda's fears soon subside when she learns that the choice belongs to God and those who lose their life for His sake, find it.

Mandy and the Mix Up $5.00

Mandy Dixon is already twenty-six and still not spoken for. Her only option in sight is her life-long friend, Clyde Anderson, but Clyde advises her to wait for God's perfect choice. Mandy wants to trust her friend's counsel, but who ever heard of Divine betrothal? And did God really have someone special picked out for her from the time she was born? Mandy's about to find out that a mix-up in her past may hold the key to her future.

Acknowledgements

First of all, I would like to thank God for giving me the desire to write, and the idea with which to form a story that I hope will be a blessing to all who read it.

Second, I would like to thank everyone involved with Local Church Bible Publishers for making the publication of this book possible. Many thanks to Mark Chartier and Santiago Lopez for their time and effort throughout the entire process. Also, special thanks is due to all the editors and proof-readers for their help, suggestions, and support.

Table of Contents

Chapter One

Heartbreak

It was early April and signs of spring were evident along every street and at every corner of the small town where the Olsens made their home. Brightly colored flowers of all sorts could be seen poking up from the moist soil and lining the walks of several houses. A gentle breeze whistled through the treetops and carried the sweet smell of freshly mown grass through the air. The late morning sun shone brightly in the cloudless sky, illuminating everything in sight with its brilliant rays.

Twittering birds sang merrily to each other outside the second story window of the Olsens' big, blue house. The window stood open, allowing the lace curtains to flutter in the breeze. The sun streamed in, warming the pretty bedroom and giving it a cheerful appearance. Everything outside was alive with the hint of new beginnings, but inside the still room, these signs of a fresh start were virtually unnoticed - overshadowed by a sorrowful ending.

Bethany Olsen lay sprawled across her bed with her face buried in pillows. Her chest tightened as her body shook with uncontrollable sobs. Her heart ached with a pain so deep she feared it could never be healed. As she saturated her pillow with tears, her pain-stricken heart screamed silent questions of despair. *Why me? Why again? Will anyone ever truly love me?*

Just an hour earlier, a young man by the name of Jack Peters had come to call on Bethany. She had been more than happy to see the young suitor with whom she had been engaged in courtship for nearly two months. However, her happiness was short lived when she realized just why he had come.

"Bethany, I am afraid I cannot court you anymore," he had said. "I feel I am being untrue to you. I'm in love with someone else." Then the gentleman had turned and walked away, leaving Bethany with another broken heart.

Bethany's first courtship had ended when the young man had decided he was not quite ready for marriage. He had eventually ended up marrying someone else, causing

Bethany even more heartache.

Her second suitor, on his way to college and realizing the great possibilities of marriage there, had decided to leave his options open. He broke off their courtship and entered college single, leaving Bethany heartbroken once again.

Now, at only twenty-two years of age, Bethany was suffering yet another heartbreak. Would she ever find someone she could trust?

Just then, there was a knock at her bedroom door. Bethany choked back her tears, swallowed hard on the lump in her throat, and mumbled, "Come in."

The door opened and Mrs. Olsen stepped in. Bethany kept her face buried in her pillows, but she knew it was her mother by the swishing sound her skirt made as she neared the bed.

"Bethany," Mrs. Olsen said, sitting down next to her. "I hardly know what to say to comfort you. I know your heart is breaking, and it's not the first time. All I can tell you is that God has someone out there for you. You just haven't found that special person yet."

Mrs. Olsen gently smoothed Bethany's golden hair out of her face as she turned to look up at her mother.

"Oh, Mom!" she moaned, fresh tears stinging her eyes. "Why does it have to hurt so much? Why can't I just find the right person without having to go through so much heartache first?"

"Honey, marriage is a big decision. It's a major commitment. It doesn't happen overnight. You have to give God time to work it all out. He will bring the right person along when He's ready. You just have to trust Him."

"I wish there were some way I could know who I am meant to marry without all this guessing," Bethany said sadly. "Sometimes I wish I had just been betrothed to someone as a child. Then someone else could have done the choosing."

"What if the person who was chosen turned out to be someone you disliked? Suppose you had nothing in common with him, or you found each other to be disagreeable?" her mother asked. "Betrothal is not always a good thing. It is better to trust God than to rely on a human's choice. God loves you, and He knows you better than anyone else. He has someone out there who will be just right. You can trust Him."

"I'm just…so…tired…of making the

wrong choice," Bethany said between sobs.

Mrs. Olsen sighed, and gently rubbed her daughter's back. "Oh, Bethany," she assured softly. "I wish marriage was an easy decision, but it just isn't."

"It was for Melissa," Bethany complained, trying to swallow the lump that insisted on remaining lodged in her throat.

Melissa was Bethany's older sister. Just a year ago, Melissa had entered marriage with the first man who had ever courted her. Bethany had entered her first courtship assuming her experience would be much like that of her sister's, but soon realized she had been sadly mistaken.

"Honey, I don't know why God has chosen this difficult path for you, but all you can do is trust Him. He works things out for good to them that love Him," Mrs. Olsen said, softly. "He has an ultimate reason for everything He does. Perhaps, when the right person comes along, you will have a deeper and greater love for the special person. Having gone through these trials, you will appreciate his love and devotion even more."

Bethany rolled over onto her back and looked up at her mother. She was a slim woman with blonde hair that fell gracefully over her shoulders.

"Mom, maybe if I were as pretty as you are, someone would have married me by now," Bethany mused, mustering a smile onto her tear-stained face.

"That's a sweet thing to say, Bethany," Mrs. Olsen smiled, wiping the remaining tears from her daughter's eyes. "Just remember, it's your inner beauty that really counts. Someday, that sweet personality of yours will attract just the right person."

Bethany sat up and gave her mother a big hug. "Thank you for helping me feel better," she said as tears of gratitude filled her eyes. "What would I ever do without you!" Then she stood up and took a deep breath, allowing the fresh scent of spring coming from the open window to fill her nose and lift her spirits.

Suddenly, there was another knock at the door.

"Come in," Bethany said.

The door swung open, and Bethany's nineteen-year-old brother, Luke, poked his head in.

"I know this probably isn't the best time, but when's lunch?" he asked.

"Oh, dear," Mrs. Olsen said, standing up and looking at the clock next to Bethany's bed. "I hadn't realized how late it had gotten. I'm sorry, Luke. You must be starving."

"That's okay, Mom," Luke said. "I know this has been a hard morning for Bethany." Then he turned to his older sister. "Don't you worry, Bethany," he said. "Any guy who would lead a poor girl on like that doesn't deserve my sister!"

"Thanks, Luke," Bethany said, giving her brother a weak smile.

"Do you feel up to eating anything?" Mrs. Olsen asked. Bethany swallowed hard, took a deep breath, and squared her shoulders. She couldn't remove the heaviness she still felt in her heart, but she wasn't about to let Jack Peters ruin her day.

Thrusting his name to the back of her mind, she answered, "Maybe a little."

Chapter Two

A Secret Prayer

The next morning, Bethany woke to the soft, steady sound of a light rainfall. She turned over and watched the raindrops as they pelted the window pane and then slid down to the sill in tiny streams.

The ache in her heart reminded her of the day before. Tears sprang to her eyes as she recalled the unpleasant visit her thought-to-be future husband had made.

Bethany had been through this before, but undoubtedly, this time felt the worst. Jack had made her feel loved. He had done special things for her and said special things to her. They had shared some of the same thoughts, and had so much in common. They were all ready to serve the Lord together for the rest of their lives. He had led her to believe that she was the most special person in his life, and then, in less than five minutes, she had discovered there was someone else.

Bethany choked on a sob and let some silent tears stream down her face. She quickly dismissed the sad memories of yesterday from her mind. The pain of them was more than she could bear. It was Friday— a new day.

Bethany slipped out of bed just as the rain turned into drizzle and sunshine burst into the room. She quickly dressed, made her bed, and then picked up her Bible for her morning devotions.

Sitting down on her bed, she opened it to where her bookmark held her place. Then she settled in and began to read Genesis chapter twenty-four. In the beginning of the chapter, Abraham sent his servant to seek out a wife for his son, Isaac. On his journey, the servant came to a well of water where he knew the young women of the city would be coming to draw from. Not knowing whom he should choose, the servant turned to God and prayed that when he asked for a drink of water, the girl God had chosen for Isaac would give him a drink and then draw water for his camels also.

Before he had even finished praying, Rebekah came out and did that very thing.

No guessing there, Bethany thought. She sighed, rested her head against her headboard, and closed her eyes. *If only that could happen today, it would spare so much heartache. Isaac and Rebekah did not even know each other. It was almost like betrothal, only God did the choosing.*

Bethany smiled. *Divine betrothal*, she thought. *The servant prayed, and Rebekah walked into his path. Neither of them even knew that they would end up at the same place at the same time. God brought them together at just the right time. Rebekah wasn't even looking for a husband. Oh, if only that could happen to me!*

Bethany opened her eyes and stared straight ahead, allowing her eyes to focus on a plaque hanging above her dresser. It said, "If ye have faith as a grain of mustard seed,...nothing shall be impossible unto you."

"Matthew 16:20," Bethany read aloud.

Suddenly, something stirred inside her. Was it a stirring of courage? Or perhaps it was hope. Bethany wasn't quite sure.

What if I could have enough faith? she thought. *Would God do for me what He did for Rebekah? Would He allow me to cross paths with the right person at the right time without me even trying? Would He give me a Divine betrothal?*

Immediately, questions of doubt sprang into Bethany's mind. *What if I'm not happy with God's choice? What if He chooses someone I don't like? Could I be like Rebekah and marry someone I don't even know? How will I know when I've crossed paths with the right person? What if I have to wait for years before He brings the right person along? What if we're all wrong for each other?*

Mrs. Olsen's words of yesterday interrupted Bethany's thoughts and put her mind at ease.

"*God loves you, and He knows you better than anyone else*," she had said. "*He has someone out there who will be just right. You can trust Him.*"

Nothing is impossible with God, Bethany thought. *If He did it for Rebekah back then, He can do it for me now.*

Before she could talk herself out of it, Bethany slid off her bed and knelt down on her knees.

Lord, she prayed. *I'm tired of courtship. I've had my heart broken so many times, only you could mend it.* Tears streamed down her face as she continued. *I want a Divine betrothal like you gave Rebekah. Please choose just the right husband for me.*

Let me walk into his path at just the right time, and help me to know for certain who it is you've chosen.

Please mend my broken heart and give me the faith I need to trust that you can do anything. In Jesus' name, Amen.

Bethany opened her eyes and stood up, feeling as if a heavy burden had been lifted from her shoulders. Perhaps it was just her imagination, but the ache in her heart didn't seem quite so painful either. She felt a stirring of excitement in her soul as if something wonderful was about to take place in her life.

Filled with a sense of renewed hope, Bethany plopped back down on her bed to finish her Bible reading. Then she spent the rest of the morning assisting her mother with the necessary household duties which included cleaning, laundry and dish washing, and a little bit of straightening.

Right after lunch, Bethany stole back upstairs to her room. She sighed and sat down at the sewing machine that was always set up in the right hand corner of the tidy bedroom.

Bethany was a talented seamstress and friends from church were always hiring her to make clothes, alter, or mend something for them or someone they knew.

Today, she needed to finish sewing a dress for Mrs. Billings' daughter who was to be the flower girl in her cousin's wedding. She needed it by Sunday.

Bethany smiled, remembering how excited the little girl had been to tell every detail of what it would be like to be in her older cousin's wedding.

I wonder who will end up being my flower girl? Bethany thought. *If I ever get married...*she added. She felt a swelling in her chest, and tears threatening to return, but she quickly blinked them away. That was all behind her now. How good it felt to let God carry the burden of finding the right husband!

I just have to trust Him, she reminded herself as she carefully guided the silky, purple fabric through the machine. The quiet hum of the motor reminded her of the peace that now filled her heart, replacing the ache of yesterday.

She could hear her mother downstairs giving a piano lesson to one of her piano students, and Luke was outside mowing the lawn. As she delicately fastened little purple flowers along the sash of the dress, she wondered if her dad would make it home on time for dinner that night.

Mr. Olsen was part of a big corporation, and his office was just outside of town. Every Friday, though, he was required to travel about a three hours' drive to the nearest big city for a business meeting with his head boss. Needless to say, he was often late getting back for dinner.

Just as Bethany was putting the last finishing touches on the little dress, Luke poked his head in the doorway and said, "Dad's home, and dinner's ready."

"Okay. Thanks, Luke," Bethany replied, laying aside her sewing.

She started for the doorway and then stopped as a sudden thought occurred to her. Should she go downstairs and announce to her family that she no longer desires to court anyone, but that she is waiting for a Divine betrothal? Luke would probably just laugh, and her parents might think it was an unwise decision. Maybe she would be better off keeping it to herself, but then suppose another young man asks to court her?

I will just have to avoid anyone who seems interested, Bethany decided.

Then she headed downstairs to the dining room, resolving to keep her prayer a secret.

Chapter Three

The Stranger

"Bethany! Bethany!"

Bethany turned to see her best friend, Leah Davidson, weaving her way through the crowded church lobby Sunday morning.

Leah was slightly shorter than Bethany and had auburn hair that hung down her back in loose curls. She was wearing a light, blue dress printed with brightly colored flowers, clearly displaying her enthusiasm over the long-awaited springtime weather. She was the same age as Bethany, and the two girls had attended the church together for over ten years.

"Hello, Leah!" Bethany called, waiting for her friend to catch up with her.

"How are you this fine Sunday morning?" Leah asked when she had reached her.

Bethany smiled. "I'm fine. How are you?" she replied.

"Good. I love your pink dress. Did you make it?" Leah asked.

"Yes," Bethany answered. "I made it a few months ago, and I've been anxiously awaiting the day when the weather would be nice enough to wear it."

"Don't you just love spring?" Leah exclaimed. Then she leaned in closer and whispered, "Do you think there's any chance of a springtime wedding?" Her eyes sparkled as Bethany's face fell. She had forgotten that Leah hadn't heard.

"No," she answered as her throat tightened. "No, there's not."

"Oh, but surely Jack has realized what a good wife you would make by now," Leah said, not understanding the pained expression that had come to rest on her friend's face.

"No, Leah," Bethany began. "There's no…It's not…Jack's…He isn't…"

Leah's smile quickly faded. "You mean…it's over?" she slowly ventured.

Bethany nodded, struggling to keep the tears from flooding her eyes.

"Oh, Bethany!" Leah gasped. "I'm so sorry! I…I didn't know."

By now, Bethany could hardly control the emotions bubbling up inside her.

Overwhelmed with unwanted feelings, Bethany dashed down a hallway and quickly rounded a corner until she was out of sight or earshot of people making their way to the large auditorium for the morning church service.

Leah rounded the corner and found Bethany hunched over against the wall with her face in her hands, sobbing.

"I'm so sorry, Bethany," she said, crouching down next to her friend and wrapping her arm around her shoulders.

"It's…it's not…your…fault," Bethany choked out. "He's…he's in love…with someone else!"

"How dare he!" Leah cried, indignantly. "Did he even consider how this would make you feel? Does he even realize what he's giving up by not marrying you?"

Bethany drew in a shaky breath and wiped the tears from her face.

"He came and told me on Thursday," she said. "That's all he said. He didn't even come in."

"I can't believe he had the nerve to betray you like that!" Leah exclaimed.

"Well," Bethany sighed. "I just hope it works out okay for him and his new girl."

"How can you forgive him so quickly

after what he put you through?" Leah asked, a look of disbelief appearing on her face.

Shrugging her shoulders in resignation, Bethany replied, "I have to. What else can I do? Besides, we betray God in our actions all the time, and yet He still forgives us. I'm really trying to be more like Him."

Bethany thought about telling Leah about the decision she had made to give up courtship and trust God to give her a Divine betrothal, but she wasn't sure how her friend would react. Besides, she had decided to let it remain a secret, and so she would keep it at that.

As the pianist began to play, Leah turned to Bethany. "We need to get in there before the choir sings without us," she said. Then her eyes softened with compassion. "Are you ready? I mean...are you okay?" she asked.

"I'm all right," Bethany replied, standing up. "It was foolish of me to react this way anyhow. It's been three days since it happened, and I've asked God to help me recover from it. I'm just a little sensitive still. That's all."

"Well, I think you're doing just fine," Leah said. "I would be a complete wreck!"

Just as the two girls stepped around the

corner, they almost ran into a young man whom they had never seen before. He was quite handsome with dirty blond hair and blue eyes. He was wearing tan dress pants and a blue-checkered, button-down shirt.

"Oh, I'm sorry!" he said, realizing he had almost run into the girls. "I'm here for the morning worship service. Where is it held?"

"In the auditorium," Leah answered. "It's back this way."

The three of them walked down the hallway and through the lobby to the big double doors at the back of the auditorium.

"Straight through here," Leah motioned as she opened the door for him.

"Thank you very much," the stranger said, stepping through the doorway. Then he stopped. "Oh, I didn't even ask what your names were."

Bethany felt her stomach flutter as she realized he was staring straight at her. Something about his crooked, boyish grin gave her a feeling she couldn't quite understand.

"I'm Bethany Olsen," she answered politely, "and this is my friend, Leah Davidson."

"Well, thank you for showing me where to go," the stranger said. "I'm pleased to have met you." Then he slipped up the aisle and quickly took a seat.

Bethany and Leah hurried up to the choir loft and joined the rest of the choir just as the service began. As they were turning in their hymnals for the first song, Bethany felt Leah nudge her.

"Bethany," she whispered. "He didn't tell us his name."

Bethany shrugged. "We didn't ask him," she whispered back.

"How old do you think he is?" Leah asked.

"I don't know," Bethany answered. She was glad when everyone began singing, and she didn't have to answer any more of Leah's questions. All through the song, "Blessed Assurance", she couldn't stop thinking about the stranger. It was odd that he had asked their names but hadn't volunteered his own. Where had he come from, and what had brought him to their small-town church?

Bethany couldn't decide if she liked him or not. He seemed nice enough, but at the same time, thinking about him made her feel flustered.

She had a good view of him from up in the choir loft. She watched him as he sang along with the congregation. Was it just her imagination, or did he keep staring at her with that boyish grin?

Bethany felt herself blush as she quickly looked down at her hymnal. Why had he come today of all days?

Suddenly, a thought sprang into her mind. Could this young stranger have anything to do with the Divine betrothal she was prayerfully awaiting? Had God brought him here so that she could walk into his path? After all, she had almost literally run into him.

Bethany stared at him for a minute and then thought, *No, it's too soon. God almost never answers prayers that quickly. I mean, I suppose He could, but it's pretty unlikely. Besides, there's just something...oh, I don't know...quirky about him-this stranger from who knows where. He seems odd and immature.*

After singing an arrangement of "Christ Liveth In Me," the choir made their way down from the loft while the congregation sang one more hymn.

Bethany watched out of the corner of her eye as the stranger's gaze followed her all the way to her seat. At least he wasn't grinning this time, but why did he keep staring at her?

Bethany sat next to Luke and tried hard to concentrate on Pastor Stanfield's sermon, but it made her uneasy to know that the stranger was only three pews behind, probably watching her.

Why is he bothering me so much? she asked herself. *We've had male visitors in the church before, and I didn't even think twice about it. Is it because I'm nervous about almost running into him? Maybe it's because he wanted to know our names.* Then she stopped. *Maybe I'm afraid he's going to show an interest in me,* she thought. *I would have to tell everyone that I don't want to court anymore, and I would have to explain about Divine betrothal. I'm not ready for this so soon!*

Lord, she prayed silently. *Please help me to concentrate on the sermon this morning and stop worrying about something that may never even come to pass. Help me to forget about this stranger I don't even know, and trust that you have everything under control. In Jesus' name, Amen.*

I'll just have to avoid him, she decided.

After the service, Bethany grabbed the bag which held the flower girl's dress she had made, and went to find Mrs. Billings.

She walked down the aisle only a few feet and then stopped. A group of men and women had formed to greet the stranger and were blocking her way.

"My name is Jesse Milford," she heard the stranger say as he shook hands with one of the men.

"How old are you?" someone asked.

Twenty-two," Jesse replied. "I'll be twenty-three on June 12."

Bethany felt her heart leap into her throat. June 12 was her birthday! She would be twenty-three then! She and Jesse had been born the exact same day?

Bethany could hardly believe it. She listened as the group further questioned this stranger named Jesse.

"What kind of work do you do?" one of the deacons asked.

"I just recently started working for a guy who builds houses," Jesse answered. "He's giving me on-the-job training."

"So, do you live right around here?" one of the women asked.

"No, I'm actually from Ohio," Jesse replied.

"What brings you here to Michigan?" a gentleman asked.

"We were hired to build a house up

here."

"How did you hear about our church?" someone else asked.

Bethany silently wondered if Jesse was growing tired of being battered with questions by this overly friendly group, but he seemed not to mind at all.

"Someone left a flyer on my hotel door," he explained. "It announced that you would be having special meetings this week, so I thought I would come check it out."

"That's right," a woman said. "The special speaker is arriving tonight and the meetings last until Friday night. Will you be attending all of them?"

"I'm planning on it," Jesse replied, with a confident nod. "I really enjoyed the service this morning. You folks have a good church here."

Just then, Bethany felt a tap on her shoulder. She had been so engrossed in listening to the conversation, she hadn't heard anyone approach her. She jumped and spun around to face Mrs. Billings.

"Oh, Bethany. I'm sorry," she apologized. "I didn't mean to startle you. I just wondered if you finished the dress for Katie."

"Oh, yes!" Bethany said, holding up the

bag with the dress inside. “I’m sorry I didn’t come and find you,” she added, feeling ashamed with herself that she had lingered so long.

“That’s all right,” Mrs. Billings assured her. “Thank you so much.” She handed Bethany the money she owed her and then turned to leave. “I have to go,” she said. “See you tonight!”

“Bye!” Bethany called. Turning to leave as well, she glanced back once more over her shoulder. As she did, her eyes met Jesse’s, and she felt her face turn red. He was staring at her again…and grinning!

Chapter Four

Dinner Guest

"What? Jesse Milford is coming for dinner?" Bethany took a stock pot from the kitchen cupboard and began peeling and cutting potatoes into it. "Why?" she asked.

It was late Monday afternoon and Bethany was helping her mother prepare dinner before the seven o'clock special meeting that night.

"Why wouldn't he?" Mrs. Olsen asked, opening the oven to take a peek at the slowly roasting chicken. The mouth-watering aroma filled the kitchen, and the warmth of the oven burst into the room.

"Well, because," Bethany started, suddenly feeling flustered. "We hardly know him."

"Luke talked to him for a while last night," Mrs. Olsen told her. "They really seemed to hit it off. Besides, your dad thought this would be a good way to welcome Jesse into our church," Mrs. Olsen explained. "It has to be hard coming into a church where you don't know anybody." She looked sympathetic as she dumped a couple bags of frozen carrots into a pan and placed them on the stove. Bethany filled her pan with water and then continued to peel and cut potatoes into it.

"He doesn't even live in Michigan, though," she continued to protest. "He will only be going to our church until he's finished with his job here."

"Well, I realize that," Mrs. Olsen said, "but we still need to make him feel welcome in the short time he is here." Then she frowned. "You almost sound as if you don't want him to come over. That's not like you, Bethany."

Bethany was at a loss for words to describe the emotions that were now swirling around inside her. How could she explain to her mother that Jesse made her nervous? How could she explain that she was afraid he might show an interest in her? How could she explain that if he did decide he wished to court her, she would have to say no, because she was waiting for a Divine betrothal?

Finally, she said, "I guess he might enjoy

the fellowship with Luke."

About half an hour later, there was a knock at the front door. Mr. Olsen had not yet arrived home from work, and Luke was upstairs, busy with his computer.

"Bethany, would you answer the door please?" Mrs. Olsen asked, carving the tender chicken and placing large slices on a serving platter. "Luke probably didn't hear it."

Bethany obediently left the kitchen and made her way to the front door, doing everything she could to quell the unruly butterflies rising in her stomach. How did she end up having to answer the door? Her heart beat wildly as she swung open the door.

"Hello," Jesse said with his crooked, boyish grin. He chuckled nervously and looked down at his feet. "At first I thought I might have the wrong house," he said, lifting his head. "I can be terrible with directions sometimes!" He laughed again nervously.

He's shy, Bethany thought to herself. Suddenly she didn't feel quite as nervous as she had a moment ago. Somehow it put her mind at ease to know that he was just as nervous about the visit as she was.

"Why don't you come in?" she invited, her face relaxing into a smile. She moved aside as Jesse stepped through the doorway. "My mother is in the kitchen preparing dinner, Luke is upstairs in his room, and my dad isn't home from work yet, but he should be home any time now," she informed him all in one breath.

Jesse nodded, but said nothing. He seemed to be taking in his surroundings with unique interest, looking all around him at the neatly decorated entrance way. He turned to his right and glanced inside the living room doorway. His eyes seemed to scan every inch of the comfortable room - from the cozy fireplace at the far end, to the intricately carved, upright piano sitting against the opposite wall. He even seemed to be noticing the framework and design of the house.

Suddenly, Bethany remembered his job was to build houses. Of course he would be interested in the way a house had been constructed.

"You have a real nice home here," he finally said, turning back to Bethany.

"Thank you," Bethany replied, shifting her feet uneasily. She silently wondered if she should invite him to sit down in the living room or if she should just bring him straight through the kitchen to the dining room. She knew one thing for sure. She certainly couldn't leave him standing in the entrance way all night!

Just then, Mrs. Olsen came hurrying through the kitchen doorway and relieved Bethany of the unspoken decision.

"Hello, Jesse," she said. "I'm so glad you were able to make it. Luke will be pleased to have a friend to talk to at the dinner table. Luke!" she shouted, turning to the staircase. "Jesse's here! Come on down!"

Bethany noticed that Jesse seemed a bit nervous again. He grinned shyly and said, "Thank you for inviting me to dinner tonight, Mrs. Olsen. It's very kind of you."

"Oh, it's no problem at all," Mrs. Olsen quickly assured him. "Come on in," she said, leading the way through the kitchen. "The dining room is straight through there, and everything is ready. Mr. Olsen should be home any minute now."

"Hey, Jesse," Luke said, following them through the kitchen doorway. "Sorry I didn't come down right away. I didn't realize you were here."

"Oh, that's okay," Jesse said, shrugging

his shoulders. He seemed to relax as Luke entered the kitchen.

"Wow, it smells good out here!" Luke exclaimed, picking at the platter of steaming chicken.

"Luke!" Mrs. Olsen scolded. "Can't you wait five minutes?"

"I'm starving!" Luke protested.

"Well, why don't you help Bethany and me carry this food out to the table, and we can all sit down."

Luke picked up the platter of chicken, Bethany took the heaping bowl of mashed potatoes, and Mrs. Olsen took the bowl of carrots.

"I can get the rolls," Jesse offered, picking up the plate of warm dinner rolls.

"Well, well! Looks like I'm just in time," Mr. Olsen said, appearing in the doorway. He followed the party to the dining room and sat down at the long oak table which had been carefully set and decorated upon Mrs. Olsen's insistence that everything be just right for their guest.

"Thank you for inviting me over, Mr. Olsen," Jesse said, taking the seat Mrs. Olsen offered him.

"We're glad to have you," Mr. Olsen replied, as Luke and Mrs. Olsen took their seats.

Bethany hesitated a moment. The only seat left was the one around the corner from Jesse! True, she wouldn't exactly be sitting right next to him since she was on an end and he on a side, but still it made her a slight bit nervous. No one seemed to notice her hesitation, so not wanting to cause a scene or seem rude to their guest, she quickly slid into the chair.

Mr. Olsen asked the blessing on the food, and then they all began passing the dishes around the table.

"How old did you say you were, Jesse?" Mr. Olsen asked, taking a bite of his dinner roll.

"I'm twenty-two," Jesse answered.

"You're the same age as Bethany then," Mrs. Olsen said, smiling. "When will you be twenty-three?"

Oh, no, Bethany thought, feeling her face grow red. *Now Jesse will know we share the same birthday!*

"I'll turn twenty-three on June 12," Jesse said.

All three Olsens turned to stare at Bethany in surprise.

"Why, that's Bethany's birthday!" Mrs. Olsen said.

"Oh, is it?" Jesse said, looking equally surprised at Bethany. "How old will you be?"

"I...I'll be twenty-three...too," Bethany said, slowly.

Jesse stared at her in silence for a moment and then said, "You mean we were born the same exact day? Wow! I...I've never met anyone before who had the exact same birthday as me. That's...that's amazing!"

"It's weird!" Luke offered, helping himself to some more chicken. "So, how's the house coming along?"

"Oh, it's coming along real good," Jesse replied.

"How long were you here in Michigan before you heard about our church?" Mr. Olsen asked, curiously.

"A couple of weeks," Jesse replied. "I've been attending a church not too far from here, but the preacher is a little hard to follow. Once in a while, he almost seems like he's not sure what he believes."

"That's too bad," Mr. Olsen said.

They were quiet for a few minutes as everyone continued to enjoy the delicious meal. Then Jesse broke the silence.

"I noticed the piano in your living room,"

he said. "Who plays?"

"Bethany and I do," Mrs. Olsen answered. "I also give lessons. Do you play?"

"Yes, I do," Jesse said. "I've taken lessons since I was seven."

"Bethany sings solos too," Luke volunteered. "She's really good at it."

"Now there's one thing I can't do!" Jesse laughed. "There is a lady in my church in Ohio who sings solos though. I accompany her on the piano sometimes."

As the dinner came to a close, Bethany began to feel more and more comfortable around Jesse. She rather liked his crooked grin, and he was really nice. Luke definitely enjoyed his company, and the evening had been a pleasant one.

Besides, Bethany chided herself. *I can't be a nervous wreck around every guy I meet, just because I'm afraid he will want to court me. I need to remember that everything is in God's hands.*

Bethany marveled at how much she and Jesse were alike. The more she learned about him, the more he seemed to have in common with her. So far, they shared the same birthday, they both played the piano, they had both been homeschooled from kindergarten through twelfth grade, and they had both asked the Lord to save them at six years old, but had later been convicted of their need to truly repent and call upon the Lord with all their heart.

Later that evening, as Jesse and the Olsens attended the seven o'clock special meeting together, Bethany still secretly hoped that Jesse wouldn't read into the fact that they were so much alike and think they were meant for each other. They did have an awful lot in common. Was it more than just a coincidence?

Chapter Five

Divine Betrothal

As soon as they arrived home from church that night, Bethany started up the stairs to her room, feeling light-hearted and happy. The worries that had plagued her earlier that evening had all been erased. She smiled. Jesse was much too kind and easy-going to be looked at as a threat. He was just a nice friend for Luke.

"Bethany," Mr. Olsen said.

Bethany stopped midway up the stairs.

"Come into the living room, Honey. I need to talk to you a minute."

Bethany descended the stairs and followed her dad into the living room. After they had both been seated across from each other, she asked, "What is it, Dad?"

"I know we haven't known him for very long at all, but…Jesse has asked my permission to court you."

Bethany's heart skipped a beat and then began to pound uncontrollably.

No! How could this be? she thought. *Just when I decide to stop worrying! What will I do now? I'll have to explain my secret, and I'll have to say no.*

"What…what did you tell him?" she asked, weakly.

"I told him that I would need to talk to you first," Mr. Olsen replied.

Bethany let out a slight sigh of relief. "How could he want to court me so soon?" she asked. "He hardly even knows me."

"Bethany," Mr. Olsen began slowly. "Jesse is quite impressed by you. He told me about Sunday morning when you and Leah Davidson helped him find the church auditorium. He said that every time you have talked to him, you have been very helpful, kind, and gracious. He also admires the humble and submissive lifestyle you have chosen - to stay at home, help your mother, sew for people - and your willingness to serve the Lord with your talents."

"He said all that?" Bethany asked. She was almost won over by Jesse's admiration for her, but Jack Peters had also once claimed to be impressed by her submissive lifestyle.

"He also feels that God is showing him

that you are the one he is meant to marry," her dad continued.

Bethany's head shot up and a slight frown creased her forehead.

"How… what makes him think that?" she asked.

"Well, you have to admit that it is almost uncanny how much you two have in common," Mr. Olsen pointed out. "Jesse told me that he has been praying hard that if God wanted him to be married, He would show him clearly who he should choose. He believes it is you."

Bethany sat in silence. What could she say? Was Jesse the right person for her? Was God bringing them together? How could she be sure? After all she had been through, she was sure of only one thing. She could not face another rejection. With this realization weighing heavy on her heart, Bethany dropped her face into her hands and began to weep.

At the same time, Mrs. Olsen and Luke entered the room. Luke sat down quietly next to his dad, and Mrs. Olsen asked, "Did you tell her?"

Mr. Olsen nodded, and Mrs. Olsen walked over and sat down next to her sobbing daughter.

"Bethany," she said, putting an arm around her daughter's trembling shoulders. "We thought you liked Jesse."

"I...I do like Jesse!" Bethany sobbed. "I just don't think...I'm...ready for this. I can't let Jesse court me."

"But Jesse is such a fine gentleman, and a sweet boy," Mrs. Olsen objected. "He has a stable job and a close relationship with the Lord. He's everything you could ever want in a husband.

"Besides, you have so much in common with him. I mean, I can't believe you were born the exact same day. There's something really special about that. You both play the piano. Why, he could accompany you with your solos! Wouldn't that be fun? It just seems that you two are meant for each other."

Bethany shook her head. This just wasn't what she had prayed for. She had prayed that God would give her a Divine betrothal - not another courtship that may or may not work out.

God, why are you doing this? she prayed silently. *This is exactly what I wanted to avoid. Please help me! Help me to know your will.*

"I'd really like Jesse as a brother-in-law,

if that helps any," Luke quietly offered.

Bethany looked up at him and smiled. "I'll keep that in mind, Luke," she said. Then she took a deep breath. "I just think I need more time."

"Bethany, no one is asking you to marry Jesse tomorrow," Mr. Olsen said. "He only asked if he could court you. That will give you time."

"But I've already been courted by three people and look what happened!" Bethany wailed, fresh tears flooding her eyes and spilling down her cheeks. "I can't bear another rejection!"

"Rejection," Mrs. Olsen said, stroking Bethany's hair soothingly. "Is that why you're afraid to allow Jesse to court you?"

"Yes," Bethany choked out. She might as well admit it. There was no other reason to say no to someone as nice as Jesse Milford.

"Bethany, you can't let the fear of rejection stop you from being sensitive to God's will," Mr. Olsen offered, gently. "What if Jesse is the one the Lord has chosen for you, and you turn your back on him. Jesse seems to be certain that you are God's choice for him."

"Besides," Luke added, "Jesse seems

trustworthy. I don't think he'd betray you like those other guys did. He's serious about this."

"I think it would be wrong of you not to at least give him a chance," Mr. Olsen said. "I think Luke is right. He is very serious about this, and it could very well be the Lord's will. You'll never know if you don't give it a chance."

Bethany sighed. Her parents were leaving her no choice. She was pretty sure they would never force her to marry or even court Jesse if she made it very clear that she had no desire to do so. But they would spend the rest of their lives thinking she was not submissive to the Lord's leading in her life. Unless she shared her secret, they would always think that the only reason she had turned Jesse down was the fear of rejection. She couldn't let them go on thinking that. She would have to explain the true and main reason for denying Jesse the privilege of courtship.

"I…I am a little hesitant to say yes to courtship again after all I've been through, but there…there's something else," Bethany said reluctantly.

"What is it, Honey?" Mrs. Olsen asked, with genuine concern in her eyes.

"A couple days ago, I made an important decision in my life," Bethany continued. "I no longer believe in courtship. I think it is nothing more than a hurtful, guessing game. The day after Jack Peters came and announced that he was breaking off our courtship, I sat down to do my morning devotions. I was reading in Genesis chapter twenty-four. After reading about how God brought Abraham's servant and Rebekah together at just the right time, and how He showed the servant so clearly that Rebekah was the right choice for Isaac, I wanted that for myself." Her voice cracked and tears welled up in her eyes as she struggled to continue her story.

"I wasn't sure if God would do something like that today until I noticed the plaque on my bedroom wall that says, 'If ye have faith as a grain of mustard seed… nothing shall be impossible unto you.'

"Suddenly, I knew that if I could just have enough faith, God would give me a Divine betrothal. That's what I called it. When God chooses two people for marriage and brings them together in a Divine way, they have experienced a Divine betrothal. That's what I've prayed for, and that's what I'm waiting for."

Bethany lowered her head. "That's why I don't want Jesse to court me."

No one spoke for a few moments, and then Mr. Olsen said, "How do you know God hasn't brought you and Jesse together in a Divine way? After all, he's all the way from Ohio. What are the chances of someone from Ohio ending up at our little church in Michigan? Isn't that what you mean by a Divine betrothal?"

"Well, kind of," Bethany replied, feeling flustered. "I...I don't know. I guess I feel like I'm standing at the well, but I'm still waiting for the sign. The servant knew Rebekah was the right girl when she gave him a drink and offered to draw for his camels, too.

"I mean, God could have brought Jesse to our church for some other reason. Maybe he just needed to be uplifted by our special meetings."

"What exactly are you looking for?" Luke asked, giving her a puzzled look. "I mean, how 'Divine' are you expecting this betrothal to be?"

"Divine enough that I know it's not either of us working it out ourselves, and
Divine enough that there couldn't possibly be any coincidences," Bethany answered

matter-of-factly. "I want it to be God's choice and no one else's."

Chapter Six

Avoiding Jesse

It was close to midnight before Bethany got to bed that night, and still she could not sleep. She found herself tossing, and turning, and fretting well into the wee hours of the morning.

How would Jesse feel, being denied the opportunity to court her? Would he be angry or upset? Would he understand? What if he never spoke to her again?

"Please tell Jesse that I must say no to courtship right now. I am waiting for God to work something out," Bethany had finally told her dad.

Now she lay restlessly in bed, worrying about Jesse, and the way he would react when he was kindly informed that there would be no courtship between him and Bethany. Would he ever forgive her?

After a couple hours of tossing and turning, she finally fell into a fitful sleep.

The next day was Tuesday, and Bethany

was scheduled to sing a solo at the special meeting that night. Her mother was to accompany her on the piano, and that afternoon, they were both in the living room, going over the song once again.

"All right. Let's do it one more time," Mrs. Olsen said, sitting at the piano. "I'm afraid that will have to do. I am suddenly feeling very achy and tired. After this, I think I will lie down, so I will be rested up for tonight's service."

"Are you sure you're feeling okay, Mom?" Bethany asked. She stood beside the piano, songbook in hand.

"Oh, yes," Mrs. Olsen assured her. "We were up quite late last night. I'm sure that's all it is." She smiled. "I'm not as young as I used to be," she added. "Now, let's start from the top."

Mrs. Olsen played an introduction, and then Bethany sang "Saviour, Like a Shepherd Lead Us" in her sweetest and clearest voice.

"I think that was your best yet," Mrs. Olsen praised when they had finished. "I'm sure you will do fine tonight. Just remember, you're doing it for the Lord. Don't worry about the crowd, or the mistakes you might make. Just sing your best for Him."

Bethany smiled down at her mother. "Thanks, Mom," she said. "You're always such an encouragement to me." Then she frowned. "You do look pretty tired. You had better go lie down. Don't worry about dinner either. I'll take care of it. You just rest as long as you need to."

"Thank you, Honey," Mrs. Olsen said, standing up from the piano bench. "I really need to get my strength back for tonight. I don't want to miss being your accompanist."

"Well, if for some reason you're not able to play for me tonight, Mrs. Baker is always willing to fill in," Bethany assured her.

By the time dinner was over that night, it had become clear that Mrs. Olsen would not be able to make it for the church service. She had developed some type of flu and would remain in bed for the evening.

Bethany made sure her mother had plenty of blankets, a glass of water, and anything else she might need, before leaving the house with her dad and Luke.

Once at church, the Olsens found their seats, and then Bethany scanned the auditorium for any sign of Mrs. Baker, the church pianist. Not seeing her anywhere, Bethany hurried up to the song leader, Mr.

Andrews.

"Mr. Andrews, do you know if Mrs. Baker will be here tonight?" she asked him.

"No, she won't be," the middle-aged song leader answered. "She's at home with a bad cold. I was just about to go find your mother and ask her if she could fill in for us tonight."

"Oh, well, my mother isn't here either," Bethany said. "She's home sick too."

"I'm sorry to hear that," Mr. Andrews said. "I don't suppose you would be willing to do it, would you?"

"Of course I would," Bethany said. "It's just that I'm scheduled to sing a solo tonight, and I need someone to accompany me. I'm not quite talented enough to play for myself."

"I see," Mr. Andrews said, slowly.

Just then, Bethany heard from behind her, "I'd be willing to accompany you."

Bethany spun around to see Jesse Milford standing a few feet away. He stepped a little closer.

"I'm sorry," he said. "I didn't mean to listen in on your conversation, but I happened to be walking by and overheard you're in need of a pianist."

"You can play the piano, son?" Mr.

Andrews asked.

"Yes, I can, Sir," Jesse answered.

"Would you be willing to play for the entire service as well as Bethany's solo?"

"Oh, well, if Bethany wanted to play for the service, I wouldn't want to take that from her."

Finally finding her voice, Bethany said, "Oh, no. That's fine. I…I don't really play all that well anyway."

"All right. Then it's settled," Mr. Andrews concluded. "Thank you very much." With that, he turned and walked away leaving Bethany with Jesse.

Suddenly, Bethany felt awkward and nervous. Had her dad talked to Jesse yet? Did he know that she was refusing to allow him to court her? How did it end up that he would be accompanying her solo anyway? Her mother and Mrs. Baker just happened to get sick on the same night?

Bethany had been planning to avoid Jesse. How would she avoid him now?

Then Jesse broke the silence. "What will you be singing?"

Bethany slowly looked up to meet his gaze. "I…I'll be singing 'Saviour Like a Shepherd Lead Us'," she answered.

"Would you like to practice once?" he

asked.

"Oh, no. I've practiced all day. I think I'm as ready as I'll ever be. Unless you need to practice," she added, quickly.

"No, I think I'll do all right with that song," Jesse said. "Just tell me how many times to play it through and all."

After Bethany had explained to Jesse her routine, she thanked him for being so kind as to accompany her and then turned to leave.

"Bethany," Jesse said.

Bethany stopped and turned to face him again.

"Your dad told me your decision to decline my offer of courtship," he said, quietly.

Bethany blushed, and her eyes fell to the floor. Was he upset with her?

Jesse seemed to read her thoughts. "Don't worry," he said, quickly. "I understand. Bethany, I would never want to marry you if you didn't think it was God's will for your life."

"Personally, I…I feel that God wants me to marry you, but until you feel the same way, we could never be happily married."

Bethany just stood there, pulse racing, heart pounding. What could she say? Jesse truly believed that they were meant to be married. Were they? How could he be so sure, and she so unsure? And what did he mean by 'until you feel the same way'? Was he saying he wasn't going to give up on her until she consented to courtship?

Heart pounding even harder, Bethany said, "I…I need to go sit down. I like to relax a little before I have to sing a solo. I'll see you later."

Then she turned and walked away, thinking, *From now on, I will have to try even harder to avoid him. He just doesn't take no for an answer.*

Before the service came to a close that night, Pastor Stanfield got up and said, "We are so happy that Bro. George could come and spend this week with us. He has three more nights to speak here. Now, I just thought it would be a nice gesture if we offered some refreshments after the services these last three nights. We already have some ladies who have volunteered to bring some things, but we could use some young folks who would be willing to serve the refreshments as well.

"My wife has posted a sign-up sheet in the lobby, so if you can help, just pick a night and write your name down. It would be nice if we could have three or four servers per night. That way people won't have to stand in line too long. Thank you so much."

After the service, Leah Davidson found Bethany in the lobby.

"Your solo was beautiful," she said.

"Thank you," Bethany answered.

"I didn't realize Jesse Milford played the piano," Leah went on. "Wouldn't it be neat if you two got married? You could perform duets together."

Bethany swallowed hard. "I don't think I'm ready for another serious commitment just yet," she told her friend.

"Oh, I'm sorry," Leah said, quickly. "I forgot."

They were silent for a moment, when Leah changed the subject, "Hey, are you going to help serve?"

"I was planning on it," Bethany replied.

"You should sign up for tomorrow night. That's when I'm signed up. We could serve together."

"All right," Bethany said as the two girls headed for the sign-up sheet.

"Oh, no," Leah said, reaching it first. "There's already three other people signed up with me. I'm afraid five people would be too much for one night."

"That's okay," Bethany said. "I'll just sign up for Thursday night. That's when Luke said he was going to help. Besides, Friday is all signed up for too. There's only one name written down for Thursday."

Bethany leaned in to sign her name and then stopped. That one name was Jesse Milford.

Chapter Seven

The Last Straw

Bethany groaned inwardly with dismay. Jesse was impossible to avoid. He was everywhere!

Not wanting her friend to get suspicious, Bethany reluctantly signed her and Luke's names. At least Luke would be there. Maybe he would keep Jesse occupied, and his mind off courtship.

Unfortunately, Thursday came all too soon for Bethany. Directly after the service, she and Luke made their way to the small kitchen where the refreshments had already been laid out. Jesse was there, waiting for them.

"So, what do we use to serve this stuff up?" Jesse asked as Luke and Bethany joined him behind the serving counter.

"I don't know," Luke said. "Bethany has served in here lots of times. She'll know."

Bethany took a mental note of which serving utensils would work best for each dish and then opened a small drawer to retrieve them. She handed Jesse a pie server for the cherry pie, and Luke a spatula for the chocolate cake. She would use a large serving spoon for the apple crisp. Everything else was finger food. The serving counter overlooked the large fellowship hall which had been set up with tables and chairs.

People began forming a line in front of the counter, and as soon as they had been served, they made their way to a table and sat down.

"Hello, Bethany. How are you?" one of the women asked as she held out her bowl for apple crisp.

"I'm doing fine, Mrs. Nelson. How are you?" Bethany replied, dishing up the dessert.

"Good. I'm so sorry your mother is still ill. Is she doing any better?"

"Well, she's been up and around a bit today," Bethany told her. "She's hoping to make it for the last service tomorrow night."

"That would be good," Mrs. Nelson said. "Say," she added, glancing to make sure no one else was waiting in line. "I was wondering if it would be possible for you to make me a tan skirt like the blue one you made for me. I just love it."

"Oh, sure," Bethany said.

"You still have my measurements, right?"

"Yes."

"Okay. Thank you so much!" Mrs. Nelson said, turning to join her husband at a table.

Just then, someone else stepped up for apple crisp.

"Hi, Bethany."

Bethany looked up into the face of Jack Peters.

"Hello, Jack," she answered, blushing. She lowered her head, and began to dish up his apple crisp. "This is the first I've seen you in church all week," she said, evenly.

It was true. Jack had not attended any of the meetings nor been heard from since his brief visit to the Olsen home.

"Been busy," Jack said, nonchalantly.

"Even on the Lord's day?" Bethany marveled. Still avoiding eye-contact, she pretended to push the remaining apple crisp into one side of the pan.

"I was at my girl friend's church," Jack said, defensively.

"What about the rest of the week?" Bethany asked, finally lifting her eyes to meet his gaze.

"I said I've been busy," Jack repeated, a scowl forming on his lips. "You know, that's what I love so much about Valerie. She doesn't expect so much out of me. She understands if I can't give every spare second I've got to the church.

"You were always pushing me to do more than I could handle. Don't get me wrong. I want to serve God and all, but a man's gotta make a living too. If I sat at home and did nothing but sew all day, maybe I'd spend more time doing stuff for God, too."

With that said, Jack spun on his heel and stalked off, leaving Bethany speechless.

"I can't believe you almost married that self-loving heathen," Luke exploded.

"Luke!" Bethany said, blinking at the tears that were stinging the backs of her eyes.

Jesse frowned. "Were you engaged to him?"

"Almost," Luke said, indignantly.

"Luke, please," Bethany said. "We were courting," she answered.

"If you don't mind my asking, how long ago did it end?" Jesse asked.

Bethany sighed and focused hard on the apple crisp in front of her to keep from crying.

"A week ago, today," she replied.

"His name is Jack Peters, and up until now, he's always pretended to be interested in living for God. What a faker!" Luke was furious.

"Luke, calm down," Bethany said. "Just thank God He spared me a life of misery. I'd rather be single the rest of my life than be stuck with a husband who doesn't see the things of God as important."

"At least you didn't find out after you were married," Jesse said.

Bethany shuddered at the thought of how close she had come to being fooled. It made her sick to think what could have become of her if she had entered marriage and then realized she'd been deceived.

"I have to admit, Jack really knew how to play the game," she said aloud.

Silently, she thanked God for allowing her to see His reason for keeping her from Jack. It also confirmed even more the need to allow God to choose her husband. He had known Jack's heart all along.

Bethany knew she could trust God to bring the right person into her life. She was now more sure than ever that He would give her a Divine betrothal.

"You know, Bethany," Jesse said, interrupting her thoughts. "What that guy, Jack, said about you sitting around sewing all day, was actually a real compliment. I know he didn't mean it that way, but you spend your time serving others. That's nothing to be ashamed of. Maybe it's not what Jack's looking for in a wife, but it's exactly what I'm looking for."

Bethany swallowed hard, and she could feel her ears burning. "Thanks, Jesse," she managed.

The next morning, Leah picked up Bethany and drove her to the nearest craft store. She had agreed to help her pick out the materials she would need for Mrs. Nelson's skirt.

On the way to the store, Bethany told her friend all about Jesse's request to court her, and her reasons for denying him. She also told her about Jack Peters.

"I've been wondering where he's been lately," Leah said. "I just thought he was too afraid to show his face after what he did to you."

"As for Jesse," she went on, "I like your idea of Divine betrothal. You're right. Courtship is a difficult thing to predict. Look at the kind of person Jack turned out to be. You wouldn't have known until too late if God hadn't intervened."

"I know," Bethany said. "Only God knows what a person is truly like or will be like ten years down the road. I can't tell you how much better I feel, letting God choose the right person."

"And you don't think Jesse Milford could be God's choice? He's an awfully nice guy."

"So was Jack," Bethany pointed out. "Everything Jesse is, Jack pretended to be. How can I be sure Jesse's not pretending too?"

"I guess you're right," Leah said. "It's better to leave it in God's hands."

When the girls arrived at the store, they immediately entered and began searching for the correct materials. Bethany picked out some nice tan fabric, and Leah found a matching button and zipper.

"I'm pretty sure I already have tan thread," Bethany told Leah. "I guess we're all set."

Bethany paid for the sewing items and as the two of them headed for the door, Leah stopped suddenly.

"Hey," she whispered. "Isn't that Jesse over there?"

Bethany looked in the direction her friend was pointing and stared in disbelief. It was Jesse! He stood quite a distance away from the girls and did not see them.

Bethany grabbed Leah's arm and pulled her behind a shelf.

"What on earth is he doing in a craft store?" Leah asked, frowning.

"This is the last straw!" Bethany whispered rather loudly.

"What are you talking about?" Leah asked.

"I know exactly what he's doing here!" Bethany replied. "He's following me!"

Chapter Eight

Jesse Disappears

"Following you?" Leah looked puzzled. "Why would he be following you?"

"He was standing right there when I asked you to come shopping with me last night at the serving counter," Bethany explained. "I'm sure he heard what time you were going to pick me up and everything."

"I still don't understand why he'd be following you," Leah said, perplexed.

"Ever since he asked to court me, I've been purposely trying to avoid him," Bethany confessed. "It's been impossible! Everything I try to do, and everywhere I try to go, Jesse's there! First, he offers to accompany my solo. Then he's signed up to serve refreshments on the same night as me. Now, he follows me to the craft store, and he keeps saying things to me that make me feel like he's pressuring me to marry him."

"Really?"

"Yes. Just last night he told me that I'm exactly what he is looking for in a wife."

"He said that?" Leah asked in disbelief.

"Yes, and I just know he followed me here on purpose."

"Who followed you here?"

Both girls jumped and spun around. There stood Jesse, right in front of them. He was holding two small boards and some oil base paints.

Bethany didn't dare even wonder how long he'd been standing there. Quickly recovering, she said, "You did."

Jesse frowned. "How could I have followed you here? I didn't even know you were going to be here."

"Of course you did!" Bethany cried, staring at him in disbelief. "You heard us talking about it last night. You were standing right there."

"I did hear that you were going shopping and Leah was picking you up," Jesse confessed. "I didn't hear what time or where you were going though. I was busy serving seconds."

Bethany stared at him suspiciously. Was he lying to her? Maybe he was just like Jack.

Suddenly, she thought of a new challenge.

"Why aren't you at work today?" she questioned.

"The electric company is wiring the house, and the plumbing is also going to be installed," Jesse explained. "My boss said I could take some time off since we can't do anything more 'til that's done."

"So, you're saying it's just a coincidence that you ended up in the exact same store at the exact same time as us?" Bethany asked, quizzically.

"No, I don't think it was a coincidence," Jesse said. "I think it was meant to happen. I told you, Bethany. I know it's God's will that we court."

Bethany was stunned at Jesse's boldness. She lowered her head and then looked up into his eyes.

"Well, I know it's not," she said.

Jesse looked surprised. "How?" he asked.

Bethany sighed. "Jesse," she began. "I think you should know. Jack,...he isn't the first person who's courted me. I've been courted three times." She blinked and bit her lip, turning her head away to gain control of her emotions.

"I've never been hurt more than I have through courtship," she continued. "Three times I grew to love someone, and three times I faced heart-rending rejections. I can't take it anymore. I will not court ever again! If God wants me to be married, He will have to drop someone into my lap.

"You can't court me, Jesse. I'm saving my heart for my husband, and only God knows who that is."

With that, Bethany made her way to the door, Leah trailing behind.

"Bethany, wait!" Jesse begged.

Bethany rested her hand on the door and glanced over her shoulder at him. Tears were already finding their way down her cheeks, and a lump refused to dislodge from her throat.

"I'm sorry, Jesse," she choked out. Then she burst out the door and ran for the car.

Lightning lit the sky and thunder boomed and crashed, rattling the window panes. Rain poured down in angry torrents as Bethany dressed for the last special meeting that night.

She felt uneasy and disoriented as she mindlessly slipped into a plain, blue dress and searched for matching hair ribbons. Not only was she overwhelmed with the sickly dread of facing Jesse again, but also the possibility that she was making a mistake toyed around in her mind.

Were her and Jesse meant for each other? Was it God's will that they marry? If so, why had God revealed it so clearly to Jesse and not to her? When had her married future become such a complicated mess again?

The heavy burden was back, the ache in her heart had returned, and doubts and fears had replaced the peace she had felt when she had first decided to let God choose her husband.

Bethany dropped to her knees beside her bed. It was time to turn to God once again.

Lord, she prayed. *I don't know who you've chosen for me to marry, or even if you want me to be married, but either way, Lord, I pray you would make it clear to me. If you want me to stay single, I want to stay single, and if you want me to be married, I want to marry the person you have chosen for me. Jesse seems to think it's him, but I'm not sure. If he is the one, please make it very clear to me. Somehow, help me to know for certain that you are bringing us together in a very special way, and, Lord,...help me to put aside my hurt feelings and just trust you. In Jesus' name, Amen.*

Bethany left the house that night with a renewed sense of strength. She was now ready to face Jesse. She would apologize to him for accusing him of something she couldn't very well prove.

She had also decided to explain everything to him. She had already told him about her three previous courtships and the heartbreaks to follow, but tonight she would reveal her most predominant reason for refusing courtship — Divine betrothal. Surely he would understand once he learned her truest and innermost desire to let God choose her mate.

The rain still poured relentlessly as Mr. Olsen drove the car down the wet, slippery streets toward church. Dark, storm clouds covered the entire sky, although the loud, booming thunder had subsided to an occasional, low rumble in the distance.

When they arrived at church, Bethany was almost disappointed to find that Jesse was not yet there.

He must be running late, she thought as she sat down next to her family. Lots of people were coming up to Mrs. Olsen and telling her how happy they were that she was feeling better and could make it for the last special meeting.

Bethany glanced around anxiously. It was now only five minutes until the service was to start. Where was Jesse? He had always been on time if not early. He was probably just running late, but Bethany couldn't shake the guilty feelings that plagued her. Was Jesse angry with her? Was she the reason he might be choosing to stay away tonight?

The distressing thoughts whirled around her like a swarm of angry bees, upset that she had dared partake of their precious honey.

Soon, the service began, and there was still no sign of Jesse. Bethany could hardly concentrate on the singing, and she honestly wondered how she would ever make it through the sermon. Then the special speaker approached the pulpit and announced the title of his message - "Do you really trust God?"

Bethany's heart stopped and so did every thought that had previously occupied her mind. All this time, she had been blaming Jesse for getting in the way of God's choice for her mate, but all those thoughts immediately came to a crashing halt.

She swallowed hard. Right then and

there she knew she hadn't really been putting her full faith and trust in God. Ever since she had prayed for a Divine betrothal she had done nothing but worry. She had worried about how she would know when the right person came along. She had worried that Jesse was going to ruin everything by insisting that he was the one she should marry. Just like the preacher was saying now, she had been trusting God in word but not in deed. How sinful she felt!

"Many times we ask God to take care of a need in our lives, but then instead of turning it over to Him, we still hang on to it," the preacher was saying. "Is it because we don't think He is mighty and powerful enough to take care of it? Or are we afraid that we won't like the way He chooses to handle it? Are we in any position to tell God how to run our lives? Do you really trust God?"

Bethany felt as if she had been stabbed twenty times over. She had asked God to give her a Divine betrothal, but who was she to tell Him how to bring it to pass?

As soon as the service came to a close, and the invitation began, Bethany knew exactly what she needed to do. Making her way up the aisle, she humbly dropped to her knees before the altar and silently confessed her sin of unbelief.

If only she had just given Jesse a chance, perhaps he would have turned out to be the right one after all. She wouldn't have necessarily had to agree to court him. If she had just allowed herself to get close to him, maybe God would have shown her that they were meant to be together. If only she hadn't been so untrusting!

She had allowed her own fear of betrayal to stop her from trusting and relying upon God, and now Jesse was gone! It was too late to apologize. It was too late to make reconciliation.

As Pastor Stanfield made the closing prayer, Bethany had a fleeting thought that perhaps Jesse had come late and slipped in the back, but when she turned around, he wasn't there. Without a good-bye or a trace, Jesse had disappeared.

Chapter Nine

A New Hope

"Maybe he was sick," Luke suggested as the family discussed Jesse's absence from church over breakfast Saturday morning.

Bethany quietly ate her eggs and listened to the numerous suggestions as to where Jesse could have been. Finally, she could be silent no longer.

"I think he's gone for good," she blurted out.

Her parents and Luke turned surprised faces toward her.

"Gone for good?" Luke repeated. "How do you know?"

"I...I met him in the craft store Friday morning," Bethany confessed. "I kind of...accused him of something I wasn't sure he had even done."

Luke frowned, and Mr. and Mrs. Olsen waited patiently for her to explain.

"Ever since Jesse asked to court me,

I...well...I've sort of been trying to avoid him. It didn't work though. Everywhere I went, Jesse was there, and everything I did, Jesse did. I felt like he was following me around or something."

"Oh, you mean like when we served the refreshments together?"

"Yes, and when he volunteered to play the piano for my solo," Bethany added. "Well, the night that we served refreshments, I asked Leah if she would like to pick me up on Friday morning and go shopping with me. Jesse was standing right there, and he even admitted that he had overheard part of our plans."

"Are you saying he may have followed you there?" Mrs. Olsen questioned.

"That's what I thought when I saw him there," Bethany said. "I accused him of it too. I asked him why he wasn't at work, and he said that the electric and plumbing companies were working on the house for a while, so he had some time off."

"Did he admit that he had followed you there?" Mr. Olsen asked.

"No, and he very well may not have," Bethany said, lowering her eyes. "You see, I've been wrong to treat Jesse the way I have. I...I never even gave him a chance. I ran from him and pushed him away, and it was all because I was afraid of getting my feelings hurt again. At the time, I told myself I was waiting for a Divine betrothal, but I wasn't really trusting God to do it. In my head, I knew He could do anything, but in my heart, I was afraid.

"Now, I think I may have made a terrible mistake. What if Jesse was right, and God was using all those 'coincidences' to bring us together? Now, Jesse's gone, and I will never know if he was the right one, or be able to apologize to him for the way I treated him."

"How do you know he's gone for good?" Luke asked. "Sounds to me like he's just taking some time off, and he will be back."

"Maybe you're right," Bethany said, resting her chin in her hands, "but why wasn't he at church last night if he's still here?"

"You never know," Mr. Olsen said. "As far as your mistake, Bethany," he continued. "God is often merciful enough to overlook our mistakes and give us a second chance. If it is God's will that you marry Jesse, He will make sure that you meet again."

"You really think so?" Bethany asked, looking hopeful.

"If you can trust Him," her dad continued, nodding his head for emphasis. "Do you think you can do that?"

"I can now," Bethany said. "I repented of my unbelief at the altar last night. I'm ready to trust God now. Whether it be Jesse or someone else, I'm ready for Him to bring us together in any way He sees fit. It may not be as big or miraculous as I had hoped, but as long as I know, it's all right with me."

Bethany spent the next couple weeks hoping and praying that Jesse would return, but every Sunday and every Wednesday night, she was disappointed.

Three Sundays passed, and Jesse still had not been heard from. Bethany came into church that Sunday night feeling a little down. The guilt she had been feeling for the last few weeks was weighing heavy on her heart. Even if Jesse didn't turn out to be her future husband, she wished she could at least have the opportunity to tell him how sorry she was. Would she ever see him again?

Bethany walked up to the piano to practice for her offertory she would be playing later that night. The Olsens had arrived early for church, so she had the whole auditorium to herself.

Just as she sat down and opened her book

to the right song, Pastor Stanfield came out the side door next to the piano.

"Oh, hello, Bethany," he said.

"Hello, Pastor Stanfield," Bethany answered.

"Are you going to be playing for us tonight?" the pastor asked, smiling.

"Just the offertory," Bethany replied.

"Well, while we're on the subject, I've been needing to talk to you about something. You see, there is a young man who is serving as the music director at a church a couple towns west of here. I preached at the college he was attending a few years back. That's where I first met him. We've kind of been good friends ever since."

"Anyway," the middle-aged pastor continued, "the church is quite small, and is in great need of some willing and able-bodied people to help out in the ministry."

Bethany frowned, trying to understand why her pastor would be confiding all this to her.

"You're probably waiting to hear why I'm telling you all this," Pastor Stanfield said, reading the expression on her face. "I'm telling you all this because this friend of mine, Brother Mark Spencer, called me and told me that his pastor is having an evangelist come and speak at their church a week from today. The meetings are going to last through Wednesday. The problem is that the church is without a pianist. They've been limping through all right from week to week, but Bro. Mark just thought it would be nice if they had a piano player for the special meetings. He was wondering, Bethany, if I had any willing piano players in my church that I could spare for the week.

"Well, I told him I have three - Mrs. Baker, your mother, and you. Now, I really can't spare Mrs. Baker, but I was thinking that perhaps you would like to do it. If you would rather not, I could ask your mother, but it just seemed to me like something you might enjoy."

"My, I would love to do something like that, Pastor Stanfield," Bethany said. "I feel so bad for their poor little church."

"It is a shame," Pastor Stanfield said, nodding his head in agreement.

"You say he's fresh out of Bible college?" Bethany asked.

"Yes, he just graduated last spring. He had been praying for the Lord's leading until he felt called to help out this little church in need of a music director. Yes, he's only twenty-four years old."

"He's also single," he added with a friendly wink.

Bethany felt her heart soar as the words penetrated her ears. He was only twenty-four, and he was single? She blushed at the pastor's wink.

"Well, I'll let you go ahead and practice," he said. "You let me know by Wednesday, all right?"

Bethany nodded, suddenly feeling too excited to practice. She forced her fingers to push the right keys, but her mind was elsewhere. What were the chances of her being asked to play the piano for a single, twenty-four-year-old, music director? What would he be like?

He seemed to be committed to the work of Christ and sensitive to His leading. She couldn't help but wonder if perhaps she was being led into his path for a Divine reason. It was all so exciting to think about!

People were now filing into the auditorium as Bethany picked up her music book and went to find her seat.

Thursday morning, Bethany could hardly be still. Her heart leaped every time the telephone rang.

At church last night, Bethany had assured Pastor Stanfield that she would be more than willing to assist the small church during their special meetings. The pastor had then informed her that he would be calling Bro. Spencer first thing Thursday morning to let him know. He also told her that he would give the young music director her phone number. He would probably want to call the same day and let her know what the service schedules would be like and what types of songs she should practice.

Now, Bethany was anxiously awaiting her phone call, wondering what it would be like to talk to this young man she had never met. It was early afternoon before the call finally came.

"Bethany! It's for you!" Luke called.

Bethany sprang into the living room and eagerly took the phone from her brother.

"Hello," she said.

"Hello, Bethany," a young-sounding voice responded. "This is Bro. Mark Spencer of Kingdom Of God Baptist Church. I talked to Pastor Stanfield this morning, and I was more than happy to hear that he had found someone who had agreed to be my pianist for the week. I'm sure he told you about our situation."

"Yes, he did," Bethany said. "I'm awfully sorry."

"Oh, it's all right," Bro. Spencer replied. "God has a special plan for our church, and I'm sure He will send us a piano player when He sees fit. For the time being, I'm so glad we will at least have a pianist for the special meetings. I think it will add to the whole spirit and mood of the services."

"I'm sure it will," Bethany agreed. "Especially during the invitations."

"Yes, indeed. You're exactly right."

Bethany smiled. She found it much easier to talk to this young man than she had ever imagined. For a fleeting moment, she allowed herself to wonder what he looked like.

Bro. Spencer went on to explain to her what the order of each service would be like, and what he would like her to practice.

After Bethany hung up, she immediately went to the piano and began to practice. She couldn't hardly remember the last time she had been so happy or had felt so hopeful.

Chapter Ten

Change of Plans

"Oh, John, you got something in the mail from your mother today."

Mrs. Olsen handed him a rather thick envelope. The family was enjoying the evening meal of spaghetti and meatballs, and Bethany had just finished telling her dad about the phone call she had received earlier that day.

Mr. Olsen took the envelope from his wife and opened it.

"No wonder it's so thick," he commented. "She has enclosed two train tickets."

"Train tickets?" Mrs. Olsen repeated, frowning.

"Why only two?" Luke asked, looking equally puzzled.

"Well, maybe she explains herself in the note," Mr. Olsen suggested, taking out a small piece of stationery and unfolding it.

"Dear John," he read aloud. "I am

having knee surgery on April 28, and I would be overjoyed if you would allow my granddaughters, Melissa and Bethany, to come and stay with me for a week or so. I do miss them and would enjoy their company as well as their assistance. I have enclosed two train tickets for their ride down here. Please let me know as soon as you can if this is possible and tell Lukey I'll have him come visit me sometime too. I do miss all of you greatly. With love, Mother."

When their dad had finished, Luke was blushing over the term of endearment his grandmother had placed on him, and Bethany was holding her breath at the question she was about to ask.

"When does she want us to come?" she ventured.

"Well, her surgery was today," her mother offered.

"Let's see," Mr. Olsen said, holding up one of the tickets. "Your train leaves at 2:00 P.M. this Saturday."

"I was afraid of that," Bethany said, letting her breath out in a heavy sigh.

"What's wrong?" Luke asked.

"If I go, I'll be gone during the special meetings that I have to play for."

"Oh, that's right," Mrs. Olsen said.

"You've already committed yourself."

"Could Melissa go by herself?" Bethany asked.

"I don't like the idea of sending Melissa on a train all by herself," Mrs. Olsen objected, concern playing on her face.

"Then Luke could go with Melissa," Bethany suggested.

"I don't know," Luke said. "I just started my post office job last week. I don't think my boss will let me have time off so soon."

"Bethany, I really think this is something you need to do," Mr. Olsen said, sincerely. "Your grandmother is very lonely, and besides, it will give you time to spend with your sister. We haven't seen her much since her and Jason moved up north."

Bethany's heart sank. Why did her grandmother's surgery have to fall on the exact week that she was supposed to play the piano for Bro. Spencer's church? This could be her opportunity to meet her future husband, and she was going to miss it. What would God want her to do? Would he want her to help out a needy church, or assist her lonely, helpless grandmother? Why did His plan for her always have to be so complicated?

"What about Bro. Spencer's church?"

Bethany asked. "They are really looking forward to having a piano player for their special meetings."

"Your mother can play for them," Mr. Olsen told her. "Now, I think we should call Melissa tonight and make sure she can go on the trip."

"That's a good idea," Mrs. Olsen agreed. "I'll give her a call right after dinner."

As Bethany washed the dishes that night, she listened to her mother making plans with Melissa over the phone. It sounded like Melissa would be able to go which meant Bethany would have to go too.

It's not fair, she thought. *Just when I think things are coming together, they all fall apart.*

Just then, Mr. Olsen came up beside her.

"Bethany," he said. "I saw how disappointed you were when you found out that you wouldn't be able to help out Bro. Spencer's church. I just think that this is an important thing for you to do right now. Your grandmother is not a Christian lady, and it will be good for her to see your love and care toward her. You will have other opportunities to use your talent to minister to others, but your grandmother won't be around forever. You understand, don't you?"

"Yes," Bethany answered. "But, Dad, how do you know what the right thing is to do, when God brings two opportunities into your path at the same time?"

"That is a difficult thing to figure out," Mr. Olsen agreed. "I think, when that happens though, we need to weigh it out and decide which one we're needed for most. Your mother can play the piano for the church, but your grandmother specifically requested that you come and stay with her. She seems to need you most right now."

Bethany nodded. Even if her dad was wrong, and she was meant to meet up with the music director, God would want her to submit to her dad. That would be the right thing for her to do.

Besides, she thought as she began packing her suitcase that night. *If God wants me at that church next week, He will make it happen. Maybe our train ride will be cancelled. Of course, if it is simply God's will for me to cross paths with Bro. Mark Spencer, perhaps I will meet him some other time. At any rate, God can do anything. I just need to submit to my dad and let God work out the rest.*

Saturday morning, Melissa arrived with

her luggage as planned. Nothing had changed. Bethany would travel with her sister to their grandmother's house, and her mother would get to meet Bro. Spencer and play the piano for the church's special meetings.

Oh, well, Bethany thought. *Maybe I wouldn't have liked him all that much anyway.*

"Bethany!" Melissa cried when she saw her sister come downstairs. "I've missed you so much!"

"Me too!" Bethany agreed as the sisters embraced.

"Are you looking forward to the trip?" Melissa asked, squeezing Bethany's hand.

"I'll enjoy being able to spend some time with you," Bethany answered, honestly. "It seems like so long since we've been together."

Melissa was two years older than Bethany and had dark hair like her dad.

"I know," Melissa said. "It's been hard living so far from my family."

"We're glad you're happy though," Mrs. Olsen told her daughter.

"Yes, we are!" Melissa said, her face suddenly brightening. "That reminds me. I have some exciting news. I mean, we have some exciting news. I'm expecting a baby!"

"Oh, Melissa!" Mrs. Olsen cried, giving her a big hug.

"When?" Bethany asked.

"I'm due October 13."

"Is it a boy or a girl?" Luke asked.

"I won't know that for at least another two months, Luke," Melissa replied. "We haven't decided yet if we even want to find out."

"What?" Luke cried. "How can you possibly wait nine whole months to find out?"

"That's the fun of it," Melissa exclaimed.

"Well, I want to know if I'm gonna have a niece or a nephew," Luke stated.

"Oh, Luke. You'll live!" Melissa laughed. Her eyes danced with untamed excitement.

Bethany tried to imagine what it would feel like to be carrying her very own baby. She smiled at the thought of being an aunt to a little niece or nephew. Luke was right. It would be fun to know.

At the train station, Bethany stood beside Melissa while the rest of the family waited to see them off.

The train pulled into the station right on schedule. After saying their good-bye's,

Bethany and her sister boarded the train and found their seats.

Soon they were off, and Bethany's chance of meeting the young music director was quickly erased by the clacking of the train's wheels as it sped down the tracks. She stared aimlessly out the window at the scenery streaking by. If only her grandmother's surgery could have been one week later, everything would have been perfect. Why did everything always have to work out wrong? It had seemed like the perfect situation until…

"Bethany," Melissa said, jerking Bethany from her thoughts. "Are you really that disappointed that you weren't able to play for that church?"

"How did you know that's what was bothering me?" Bethany asked, turning to face her older sister.

"I have my ways," Melissa answered, grinning.

"Well, you see," Bethany said. "There's more to it than that. I didn't exactly tell Mom or Dad about this, but the church's music director is only twenty-four, and he's single. I couldn't help but wonder if maybe God was bringing us together for a special reason."

Melissa nodded knowingly. Bethany had kept her updated over the phone on all the things that were happening between her and Jesse. Melissa knew all about Bethany's decision to put Divine betrothal above any kind of courtship.

"So, do you feel like you're out of God's will right now?" Melissa asked, searchingly.

"No," Bethany answered, shaking her head slowly. "I'm submitting to Dad. Even if playing the piano for that church was the right thing to do, it would have been wrong for me to go against what Dad asked me to do."

"I guess I'm just dying to know what could have happened," she finished, giving her sister a guilty smile.

Chapter Eleven

Peace and Comfort

Bethany's grandmother lived at the very southern edge of Michigan, and within just a few hours of travel, they arrived in her town. Of course, with it being only two days after her surgery, she was not there to greet them at the station, but a local taxi took them from the train station to her house. Inside, a nurse was caring for their grandmother who had apparently just arrived home from the hospital.

"Melissa! Bethany!" Grandma Olsen cried, holding her arms out to them. She sat in a wheelchair with a bandage and brace covering her left knee.

"Hello, Grandma," Melissa said, bending down to give the elderly woman a hug and kiss. Bethany did the same.

"It's so good to see you again!" Grandma Olsen exclaimed, holding her granddaughters' hands and looking them over affectionately.

"How are you feeling?" Bethany asked.

"Oh, a little sore is all," Grandma Olsen replied. "I'll be fine now that you're here."

"Oh, Millie," she said, suddenly turning to the young nurse, standing by. "These are my granddaughters, Melissa and Bethany."

"It's nice to meet you," Millie said, giving them a pleasant smile.

She had light brown hair and sparkling blue eyes. She appeared to be just a little older than Melissa.

"It was so sweet of you to come and stay with your grandmother like this," she said. "I'll be checking in on her once a day until she has recovered sufficiently. You can leave the bandage changing to me, and if you have any questions about anything, just let me know."

"Thank you," Bethany said. "We very much appreciate your kindness."

After leaving a few simple instructions, Millie said good-bye and left the house.

"Would you mind setting the kettle on for tea, Sweetheart?" Grandma Olsen asked, turning to Melissa. "Then we can have tea together in the kitchen, and you can tell me all about what you've been up to."

Bethany pushed her grandmother's wheelchair into the kitchen while Melissa put some water in the tea kettle and set it on to boil.

"Grandma, I have some exciting news," Melissa said as they all sat around the table to wait.

"What's that, dear?" Grandma Olsen asked, curiosity showing in her grey-blue eyes.

"I'm expecting a baby," Melissa announced.

"Oh, how wonderful!" Grandma Olsen exclaimed. "When?"

"October 13," Melissa replied. "Jason and I are so excited! We already have names for boys and girls picked out."

"Well, be sure to let me know what you're having as soon as you find out!"

"Jason and I aren't sure yet if we want to find out. We might let it be a surprise."

"So, how is your Jason doing?" Grandma Olsen inquired. "What is he up to these days?"

"Oh, he's working as a janitor for our church's Christian school. He also serves as deacon at the church."

"Well, that sounds good," Grandma Olsen declared.

Just then, the teapot began to steam. Bethany jumped up to help Melissa get the cups and saucers on the table. After the tea was poured, Grandma Olsen fixed her gaze on Bethany.

"You haven't told me much about yourself, dear. What's new with you? A new boy in your life perhaps?"

"No, Grandma," Bethany answered.

"My, I had a pretty steady relationship with a boy by the time I was thirteen," Grandma Olsen declared. "I was married by eighteen. The older you get, the harder it is to end up married you know. Aren't you a little worried, Honey?"

Bethany sighed. "Actually, I was for a while, Grandma," she admitted. "I've been in courtship relationships three times, and each time I was rejected. After that, I finally decided to say no to courtship and just let God bring the right person into my life.

"At first, I had trouble trusting in Him, but now I am sure He can do anything. I was silly to ever worry about who I would marry. God already has that all planned out. I just have to wait for Him to work it out in His time."

Grandma Olsen frowned. "How can you be so sure that God will just bring someone along without you doing some seeking yourself?" she asked.

"Grandma, do you have a Bible?" Bethany asked.

"Um, yes. It's in the drawer inside my end table in the living room," Grandma Olsen said. "Melissa, would you go and get it, my dear? Thank you."

Melissa handed the Bible to Bethany who opened it to Genesis chapter twenty-four. She then asked her grandmother if she would allow her to read it to her.

"Of course," Grandma Olsen said, leaning forward with interest.

Bethany then began to read the chapter aloud. When she had finished, she looked up to face her grandmother.

"This is the chapter I happened to be at in my Bible reading the day after I was rejected this last time," Bethany told her.

"It's a wonderful story," Grandma Olsen remarked.

"Yes, it is, Grandma," Bethany agreed, "but not only that. It is also a true story, and I believe God can do this today just as easily as He could then. He still performs miracles, and I believe He can perform this same miracle in my life that He did in Rebekah's. In fact, I've asked Him to do just that. It has taken some time for me to learn to trust Him completely, but I know it will be so rewarding in the end. God knows me better than anyone else, and it is so comforting to know that He will make the best choice. That's why I have decided to let Him give me a Divine betrothal."

"A Divine betrothal?" Grandma Olsen repeated with a frown.

"Yes," Bethany responded. "You know how parents decide to promise their children to each other for marriage, and they call it betrothal?"

Still looking somewhat confused, Grandma Olsen slowly nodded her head.

"Well, when God decides that it is His will that two people be married, and He brings them together in His Divine way, I call it Divine betrothal," Bethany explained. "It's like betrothal, only God is making the choice."

"How interesting," Grandma Olsen said, a far-away look in her eyes. "It's almost like a fairy tale. Do you really believe God could do something like that?"

"Of course I do, Grandma," Bethany said, matter-of-factly. "God can do anything. That's why it is so comforting to be able to put your trust in Him."

Grandma Olsen grew quiet for a moment. "I wish I could have the same peace and comfort in God that you do, Bethany," she finally said.

"Oh, but you can, Grandma," Bethany said. "All you have to do is trust Him as your Lord and Saviour, and He will fill you with a peace and comfort too wonderful to express with words."

"Would you like us to show you how you can be saved, Grandma?" Melissa asked.

"No," Grandma Olsen said, staring down at her folded hands.

Melissa and Bethany exchanged discouraged glances. They had been so close to winning their grandmother to Christ. Would they get another chance before it was too late?

Suddenly, Grandma Olsen spoke. "I don't need you to show me how to be saved," she said, softly. "I already know how. All I have to do is confess and forsake my sins and ask the Lord Jesus to come into my heart and cleanse me from them. If I mean it with all my heart, God will save me and give me a place in Heaven when I die."

Melissa and Bethany glanced at each other once again. They were surprised at how well she knew the plan of salvation.

"Girls," Grandma Olsen continued. "Your father has talked to me many times about being saved. I guess I've just never been able to believe that God was real enough to come into a person's heart, cleanse them from sin, and give them peace."

"That is, until I saw how real it is in your life," she added, looking at Bethany. "Your faith and trust in God is so real, it makes me want God more than I've ever wanted Him before."

"Grandma, would you like to trust Christ as your Saviour right now?" Melissa asked, hopefully.

"I...I think I'd like a little more time to think," Grandma Olsen replied slowly.

"We don't want to rush you, Grandma," Bethany said. "You have to do it when you're ready, or it won't mean anything."

"Anyone can die at any moment," Melissa added. "We just don't want you to wait until it's too late."

"I understand," Grandma Olsen said, finishing the last bit of her tea.

The next morning, Bethany awoke to the smell of breakfast cooking. It took her a moment to remember where she was. Just then, her sister entered the guest room and jogged her memory.

"Come on, Bethany. Get dressed,"

Melissa said. "I need your help in the kitchen. I want to have breakfast all ready for Grandma when she gets up."

"All right. I'll be out in a minute," Bethany promised, slipping out of bed. She quickly dressed and within minutes, joined her sister in the kitchen.

The sisters were just setting the scrambled eggs and ham on the table when Grandma Olsen appeared in her wheelchair.

"What a pleasant surprise!" she exclaimed, seeing the neatly set table. "I could smell breakfast cooking all the way from my bedroom."

"How did you sleep last night, Grandma?" Melissa asked as the three of them gathered around the kitchen table.

"To be honest, I didn't hardly sleep a wink," Grandma Olsen admitted.

"Oh, Grandma! Were you in a lot of pain?" Bethany cried.

"You should have called for us," Melissa insisted. "That's what we're here for."

Grandma Olsen shook her head slowly. "You wouldn't have been able to help me," she said, staring at them from across the table. "It wasn't my pain that was keeping me awake. It was what you said yesterday about dying. Late into the night I laid there in bed, imagining myself dying before I had the chance to ask God to save me.

"The truth is, I was afraid to fall asleep for fear I might die before morning. Finally, at four in the morning, I just let go of all my foolish doubts and reservations and asked Jesus Christ to be my Saviour."

"Oh, Grandma! That's wonderful!" Melissa cried.

"You were right, Bethany," Grandma Olsen said. "I could not have even imagined the peace and comfort that now resides in my soul. I'm no longer afraid of dying either. The wonderful Saviour your family has talked about all these years is finally my Saviour too!"

Chapter Twelve

A Divine Plan

After Melissa and Bethany had cleared the table and washed the breakfast dishes, they sat down in the living room with their grandmother for a little Bible reading.

"I'm so glad I'm saved," Grandma Olsen declared when they had finished. "I can't think if I had lived even one more day without knowing Jesus Christ as my Saviour. I'm so glad you girls were able to come and stay with me. Just think if you hadn't been able to come. I may have never gotten saved."

"Grandma, I…I have a confession to make," Bethany finally admitted. Her eyes remained focused on her lap as she spoke. "When we first received your letter and the train tickets, I didn't want to come. Not because of you, but…there were other reasons."

Bethany then proceeded to tell her

grandmother about Bro. Mark Spencer and the needy church. She explained that she had been scheduled to play the piano for their special meetings which were being held the same week the train tickets were dated for. She even confessed that she had wondered if God was working things out to bring her and the music director together for marriage.

"Oh, Grandma. The whole way here I was wondering if I was making a mistake," Bethany said, sadness filling her eyes. "I was so selfish to have ever thought that way. As if my life and my future are the only things that matter. God and His plan are much more important than anything I could ever dream up. He knew that by coming to see you, we would have the pleasure of leading you to salvation.

"Grandma, I'm so sorry for not wanting to come here. I'm so glad I listened to Dad and did the right thing. Turns out, this was God's will all along. Will you please forgive me?"

"Oh, Darling, of course," Grandma Olsen said. "You don't have to apologize. Anyone knows that meeting a young, single music director sounds much more appealing than spending a couple weeks with your ailing grandmother."

Bethany grinned, relieved to have that off her chest and surprised at her grandmother's new-found compassion and understanding. God had already begun a special work in her life.

Two weeks went by faster than Bethany had ever imagined it would. Every day, Grandma Olsen gradually healed physically and grew spiritually. Never did a day go by when she didn't look forward to her granddaughters reading the Bible with her. Even her nurse, Millie, noticed that she seemed more cheerful than usual.

On the last day of their visit, Melissa and Bethany packed up their things and placed them by the door.

"We have time to make lunch before we go," Melissa said. "Our train doesn't leave until two."

"I'm really going to miss your good cooking," Grandma Olsen said when they had sat down to eat. "I'm sure Jason enjoys it," she said, smiling at Melissa. Then she reached over to pat Bethany's hand. "And I'm sure whoever God has picked out for you will surely enjoy your cooking too, Dear."

"Thank you, Grandma," Bethany said.

Right after lunch, the girls washed the dishes and then prepared to leave.

"I wish I could come and see you off at the station," Grandma Olsen said, apologetically.

"Oh, we'll be all right, Grandma," Melissa told her. "It's been a really nice visit," she added, sincerely.

"You have no idea," Grandma Olsen said. "You will never know how much this visit meant to me."

Melissa hugged her grandmother, and Bethany followed suit.

"Good-bye, Grandma," Bethany said. "I'm going to miss you. I hope you make a complete recovery real soon."

When they arrived at the train station, Melissa and Bethany boarded the train headed north. They stored their bags in the racks above their heads and then took their seats. Within minutes, they were on their way home.

"Wasn't that the nicest visit?" Bethany asked. "I just can't believe Grandma got saved!"

"I can't either!" Melissa agreed. "Dad was so excited when she called and told him. Just think how long we've prayed for her to be saved!"

"Oh," Bethany sighed, resting her head against the back of her seat. "It's been a long and exciting couple of weeks."

"That's for sure," Melissa agreed.

Bethany dozed on and off during the first hour of the trip. She hadn't realized how tiring it had been, caring for her grandmother.

Halfway through the trip, they were given a snack and some glasses of cold water.

"I had a nice visit with Grandma, but it will be nice to get back home," Bethany said, nibbling on a pretzel. "I wonder how Luke's post office job is going."

"I'm sure he's doing just fine with it," Melissa said. "He's a good worker."

"Well, I think I'm going to take a trip to the restrooms and freshen up just a little before we reach home," Bethany said, standing up and pulling a brush from one of her bags. "I'll be right back."

Carefully, Bethany made her way down the long, narrow aisle to the restrooms at the back of the car. After washing her hands and face and straightening her hair, she slowly headed back down the aisle toward her seat.

As she passed a man reading the

newspaper, the train suddenly lurched, throwing Bethany off balance. Just as she managed to regain her footing, the man in the seat cried out.

"Look out!" he shouted.

Bethany glanced up just in time to see the bag which was stored above the man's head, slide off the rack and fly out toward her head. She ducked and was about to scream when someone from behind reached out and grabbed the tumbling luggage.

"So, you still insist you can live without me."

Bethany whirled around.

"Jesse!" she cried. "Where...how...what are you doing here?"

"I was wondering the same thing," Jesse responded, shoving the bag back on the rack. "Are you riding alone?"

"No. My sister, Melissa, is riding with me. We're returning from a two-week visit with our grandmother. She lives down by the border."

"Come on," she said, turning to continue down the aisle. "I'll introduce you."

Jesse followed Bethany to her seat and was promptly introduced to Melissa. After taking the seat across from them, he told them that he was headed back to their town as well.

"Why did you leave?" Bethany asked. "It...it wasn't on account of anything I did. Was it?" she asked, feeling a little guilty.

"Well, yes and no," Jesse answered. "I mostly left because my boss gave me some time off while the electric and plumbing were being installed in the house. I decided to go back to Ohio and visit my family for a few weeks."

"So, what was the other reason?" Bethany asked, hesitantly.

"Okay, I guess I had better tell you the whole story for this one," Jesse said. "You see, Bethany, the truth is, I've also been through three courtship relationships that didn't work out. It's not easy getting to know someone and then realizing they're not the one for you. Anyway, shortly after the third breakup, my pastor preached a message about letting God lead you to the person He has picked out for you to marry. He used the example of Isaac and Rebekah in the Bible. They didn't have to pursue anything, or work things out themselves. God just brought them together through His own power.

"That night, during the altar call, I surrendered the choice of my mate to God.

Shortly after that, my job led me to your town. For a while, I attended a church not too far from the hotel I was staying in. As you know, I wasn't real happy there, so when I received a flyer announcing the special meetings at your church, I thought I'd try it out.

"Bethany, I can't describe how, but I knew even before I went to bed Saturday night that the girl I was meant to marry was at your church. God revealed it to me, and when I walked in and met you and your friend, I just knew it was you. I can't explain it except that God was working. The more and more I got to know you, the more and more it was confirmed. We had so much in common, and the Lord just seemed to be using circumstances to bring us together."

"Then...why did you leave?" Bethany asked, confused. "If you knew...You didn't even say good-bye or...or explain."

"I couldn't. You ran away," Jesse told her. Bethany lowered her head, remembering the day in the craft store. "I knew all along that God was bringing us together, but you wouldn't believe me. That's partly why I left, to give God time to work in your heart and confirm it to you somehow."

"Oh, Jesse, He has!" Bethany said, looking up at him with tear-filled eyes. "I'm so sorry for the way I treated you. After you disappeared, I felt awful. I knew deep down inside that I had made a terrible mistake. My personal feelings and lack of trust had blinded me from seeing God's will for my life. I had no idea where you had gone, or if I'd ever see you again. I was afraid it was too late, but my dad told me if God wanted us married, we would surely meet again. He was right!"

Suddenly, something dawned on her.

"Melissa! Jesse!" she cried. "This is the Divine betrothal I prayed for!"

"A Divine betrothal?" Jesse repeated, frowning with bewilderment.

"Yes," Bethany said excitedly. "The day after Jack Peters broke up with me, I read that same story in my Bible reading that your pastor preached on, Jesse. I called it a Divine betrothal, because it was like betrothal, only God chose them for each other. That morning, I gave up on courtship and prayed that God would give me a Divine betrothal. There's no doubt in my mind that God has brought us together on this train for a Divine reason, but that's why I said no to allowing you to court me."

"Well, now that you've been given your Divine betrothal, will you please agree to be my wife, Bethany Olsen?"

"Of course I will, Jesse Milford," Bethany answered, her face brimming with excitement. "I have no doubts whatsoever that you are definitely God's choice for me. We are God's choice for each other."

"Bethany, as soon as we get back to your town, I'd like to ask Pastor Stanfield if we could begin premarital counseling," Jesse said. "You don't think it's too soon, do you?"

"Of course not," Bethany assured him. "Why should we wait when we know for sure that God has brought us together to be married?"

"That's what I figured!" Jesse said, shrugging his shoulders and giving her one of his crooked grins.

Bethany smiled back. How could she have ever been so wrong about Jesse? She was so thankful to have been given this second chance.

A few weeks later, Bethany sat down to write her Grandma Olsen a letter.

Dear Grandma,

Melissa and I arrived home safely, and guess what? I'm engaged! A little over a month ago, a young man named Jesse Milford attended our church during a week of special meetings. He lives in Ohio, but is staying in Michigan for a while on account of his job. He works for a house building company.

Anyway, during that week, he felt sure God was telling him to marry me, but I had just decided to stop courting and trust God to give me a Divine betrothal. Feeling frightened and unsure, I avoided him and put him off. Then, one day, he up and left. I soon realized I'd been wrong about him, but I was afraid it was too late. I had no idea where he had gone or why. I was worried, but Dad told me that if God wanted us to be married, He would arrange for Jesse and I to meet again.

To my surprise, I ran into Jesse on the train that was taking Melissa and me back home from our visit with you! Jesse had gone back to Ohio for a brief visit with his family and was traveling back to Michigan to resume construction on the house he's building.

Right then and there, I knew God had granted me a Divine betrothal, and just think, Grandma, you had a part in it all. It was my visit with you that allowed me to be on that same train at the same time as Jesse.

We are both so happy and confident that God is working in our relationship. Jesse officially proposed to me on our birthday, June 12. (Yes, Jesse and I share the same birthday!) We are planning our wedding for September 12; a month before Melissa's baby is due. Lord willing, we hope to see you there!

Love always,

Bethany